"Skunks! Go to Bed!"

By Ted Bailey
Illustrated by Lisa McCue

A GOLDEN BOOK • NEW YORK
Western Publishing Company, Inc., Racine, Wisconsin 53404

Winter had just come to the woods. Old Bear put on her nightgown, Chipmunk climbed into bed, and Badger blew out his candle.

But the Skunks slid on the ice. They sang silly
songs and laughed in a silly way.

"Skunks! Go to bed!" said Chipmunk. "It's winter and we all need to rest!"

"Not us!" shouted Willie, Wally, and Lulu Skunk. They banged on their drums and tap-danced on the frozen pond.

The Skunks continued to act silly and keep everyone up for the next two nights.

The rest of the animals had a meeting.

"What can we do?" asked Badger.

"Send those clowns to the moon!" yelled Chipmunk.

"No, no," said Old Bear. "We just need to put the Skunks to bed. Listen, I have a plan."

The next day Chipmunk took a note to the Skunks. It said:

WINTER PARTY
AT OLD BEAR'S HOUSE.
SKUNKS WILL PERFORM!

"Oh, boy! That's us!" said Lulu.

That night the Skunks took off through the woods, singing, "A party! A party! We love a good party!"

The Skunks had a wonderful time on the way to the party, shaking the snow off the trees and frightening the birds.

When the Skunks arrived at Old Bear's house, it was nice and cozy and warm. All the animals greeted the Skunks when they came in. Some animals were sitting around the fire; others were talking and nibbling on food.

"HI!" shouted the Skunks all at once.

Wally Skunk put a lampshade on his head and danced around the room.

Lulu told loud, silly jokes and laughed in a loud, silly way.

Willie bragged about his tap dancing and went around slapping everyone on the back.

"Time for refreshments!" called Badger as he passed around mugs of steaming hot milk. The milk made the Skunks a little sleepy, but they tried not to show it.

"Attention, everyone," said Woodchuck. "I'd
like to ask our friends the Skunks to dance."

"Yippee! A tap dance," said Willie.

"Oh, no, Willie," said Old Bear. "I only have
slow records. So please do a nice slow dance for
us—just dance on your toes."

Old Bear put on her favorite record, *Swan Lake*. The Skunks looked at each other and began to dance around the room on their toes. The Skunks grew just a little more sleepy, but they tried hard not to show it.

When the dance was over, the Skunks clapped
for themselves.

"Play faster music now," said Lulu.

"Drums!" yelled Wally.

"I'm sorry, dear," said Old Bear. "I have no
drums. I only have these three harps."

Willie, Wally, and Lulu looked at each other
and began to play the harps. They grew even
more sleepy, but that made them try even harder
not to show it.

"Let's sing a song now," said Badger.

"'Jingle Bells'!" said Lulu.

"I'm sorry, dear," said Old Bear. "But we only know the words to 'Rock-a-bye, Baby.'"

The Skunks stood up and sang very loudly: "Rock-a-bye, baby! Oh, baby! Oh, baby!"

"Dear ones," said Old Bear gently, "let's sing the song a little softer, and let's sing the right words, please."

So the three Skunks sang very softly.

"Rock-a-bye, baby, in the treetops..." As they sang, their little skunk heads began to droop.

"When the wind blows, the cradle will rock..." And their eyes began to close.

"When the bough breaks, the cradle will fall..." Soon the Skunks were sitting on the floor.

"Down will come baby, cradle and all." At last the Skunks were sound asleep.

The animals put blankets over the Skunks
and pillows under their sleeping heads.
    "Good night, silly ones!" said Old Bear. "See
you in the spring."
    After everyone went home to bed, the woods
were finally quiet…

except for some very loud snoring.